P9-CLZ-842

Uh-oh, Cleo

I Barfed on Mrs. Kenly

Jessica Harper

ILLUSTRATED BY

Jon Berkeley

G. P. Putnam's Sons
An Imprint of Penguin Group (USA) Inc.

G. P. PUTNAM'S SONS
A division of Penguin Young Readers Group.
Published by The Penguin Group.
Penguin Group (USA) Inc., 375 Hudson Street, New York, NY 10014, U.S.A. Penguin Group (Canada), 90 Eglinton Avenue East, Suite 700, Toronto, Ontario M4P 2Y3, Canada (a division of Pearson Penguin Canada Inc.). Penguin Books Ltd, 80 Strand, London WC2R 0RL, England. Penguin Ireland, 25 St. Stephen's Green, Dublin 2, Ireland (a division of Penguin Books Ltd.). Penguin Group (Australia), 250 Camberwell Road, Camberwell, Victoria 3124, Australia (a division of Pearson Australia Group Pty Ltd). Penguin Books India Pvt Ltd, 11 Community Centre, Panchsheel Park, New Delhi - 110 017, India. Penguin Group (NZ), 67 Apollo Drive, Rosedale, North Shore 0632, New Zealand (a division of Pearson New Zealand Ltd.). Penguin Books (South Africa) (Pty) Ltd, 24 Sturdee Avenue, Rosebank, Johannesburg 2196, South Africa. Penguin Books Ltd, Registered Offices: 80 Strand, London WC2R 0RL, England.

Design by Richard Amari. Text set in Eco 101.

Library of Congress Cataloging-in-Publication Data
Harper, Jessica. I barfed on Mrs. Kenly / Jessica Harper ; illustrated by Jon Berkeley. p. cm. — (Uh-oh, Cleo) Summary: When Cleo has a bout of carsickness on her way to a birthday swimming party, she is terribly embarrassed, but her friend's mother helps her to forget the incident by encouraging Cleo to show off her talent for diving. [1. Sick—Fiction. 2. Embarrassment—Fiction. 3. Diving—Fiction. 4. Family life—Illinois—Fiction. 5. Winnetka (Ill.)—Fiction.] I. Berkeley, Jon, ill. II. Title. PZ7.H231343Iab 2010 [E]—dc22 2009003920
ISBN 978-0-399-24673-9
1 3 5 7 9 10 8 6 4 2

For Liza.

JH

For Mum,
who was no stranger to
baby barf in her time.

JB

Chapter 1

The thing about Mrs. Kenly is, she doesn't deserve to get barfed on, especially not when she's wearing a fur coat.

Of course it had to be me who barfed on her.

I mean, some parents, well, you wouldn't feel a hundred percent sorry if you threw up on them. (Like Mrs. Landon. She laughed at me that time I had toilet paper stuck to my shoe.) But whenever I go to my friend Katy's, Mrs. Kenly gives us these huge chocolate chip cookies she keeps in the freezer. "Here ya go,

kidlets," she'll say. Then she'll sit and ask you how school was and everything. Not for hours, so you'd get bored or embarrassed, just long enough. Or sometimes she takes us to the movies. You know she doesn't really want to see some movie about a princess or a dolphin or whatever. But she'll take us any-way and act interested.

I mean, Mrs. Kenly SO doesn't deserve to get barfed on.

What happened was, we were going to Courtney Kling's birthday party and it was cold. I mean it was about a thousand below zero. If you stepped outside in your party coat like I did, you'd start shivering in one minute. So it was kind of weird and fun that the party was all about going swimming.

Mrs. Kling belongs to a special club that has this indoor pool; even when it's a thousand below, you can put on last summer's bathing suit and dive in. Meanwhile, right outside, people are walking around with steam coming out of their noses.

In the summer, we go to a pool near our house and swim like mad, every day. Plus, I take diving lessons from Mr. Jarvis. He is really tan because he's ALWAYS in the sun showing kids how to dive. Also, he has a REALLY hairy chest (not from the sun, of course). When he puts his arms around you

to show you the right position, it's like you're getting a lesson from a bear.

I've learned four tricks so far: I can do a

flip and I can do a handstand on the edge and then dive in. Also, I can do a swan dive or a jackknife.

"There ya go, Ariel!" Mr. Jarvis'll say after a good dive. He calls me Ariel, like the Little Mermaid from that old movie. "Born to swim, ya were, Ariel, born to dive!" he'll say, with a pirate accent. When people call me Cleo, my regular name, he looks confused.

Mr. Jarvis thinks I could be an Olympic diver if I want. "There's gold in your future, Ariel, gold!" he'll say. But the trouble is, when I try to dive backward, I feel like I'm lost in space. I flop on the water in some awful position, SMAPP! Plus, I can't help it—I yell. The whole thing is just too embarrassing for words. So I don't think I'll be in the Olympics because you have to be able to dive backward without SMAPPing or yelling. I'll just keep doing my four tricks, over and over. And that's fine. I'm happy with my four tricks.

Anyway, back to Mrs. Kenly and her fur coat.

Chapter 2

See, in Winnetka, Illinois, some people (ladies, mostly) wear fur coats because, like I said, it's awfully cold in the winter. I know it's a little weird—let's face it, a fur coat is made of small brown animals. (Usually minks.) But me and my little sister, Lily, like it when my parents have a winter party and the fur coats show up. Then we get to play Dainty Ladies at the Ball, like we did on New Year's Eve.

We got two fancy glasses and two napkins and a plate of party food from the kitchen. We sneaked into my parents' bedroom, where the party people put their coats. Mrs. Shell and Mrs. Landon and Mrs. Bulger all wore fur that night; the pile on the bed looked like a bunch of dead animals with a few coats mixed in. We laid out our little party, talking like Dainty Ladies at the Ball: "*OOOOOH*, *haallllooo*, Mister Creampuff, *SOOOO* nice to *SEEEE* you!" (We knew about the Dainty Ladies from watching the movie *My Fair Lady* about a billion times.)

We borrowed high heels from Mom's

closet and then we each chose a fur coat. Mine (Mrs. Bulger's) smelled like perfume. It

was all silky inside, so it slid around over my pajamas. Lily picked Mrs. Shell's because it was short, a jacket, so it only went to her knees instead of dripping on the floor like mine.

We used straws for pretend cigarette holders, even though I don't think anyone actually smoked at the *My Fair Lady* ball. They didn't smoke at the party downstairs either, except for Mr. Bulger. He went outside with a cigarette about every five minutes. You could tell which coat was his because it smelled gross, like ashes.

We ate mini-wieners wrapped in crust

and snowman cookies with our little fingers stretched out. (That's how Dainty Ladies do it.)

"Oh, it's simply delicious, isn't it, *dahling*?" I said.

"Oh, yes, *mmm*," said Lily. She's only four. I like playing with Lily because I can be the boss of her. If I played Dainty Ladies with my big sister, Jenna, I would DEFINITELY NOT be the boss.

I made Lily check about every ten minutes to see if the guests were eating dessert. When they were, we rushed to put everything back. Then we went to play James Bond with Jenna and my twin brother, Jack. We sat at the

top of the stairs with binoculars, spying on the guests.

But let's get back to Mrs. Kenly.

Chapter 3

Mr. Kling was driving a van to the party. I got the middle seat in the middle row, all squished in. Unlucky Mrs. Kenly got stuffed in next to me. Her beautiful fur coat splashed across my lap when she sat down, *fumpf*.

The thing is, I always get carsick. When we drive to my grandfather's house in the country, we have to stop a couple of times so I can get out and either throw up or just wait till the throw-uppy feeling goes away. My mother always brings a plastic bag just in case.

She sings her barf song:

"Always be prepared before you
Venture out the door.
For if you're not, then what you've got is
Throw-up on your floor!"

I was NOT prepared when I got in the van with Mrs. Kenly. No bag and all squished in.

Plus, Mom had made pancakes that morning, like she usually does on Saturdays.

When I got downstairs, she was already on batch number two. She was singing her pancake song:

> *"Hey, butter, batter, butter, ssssss, flip flap,*
> *Hey, butter, batter, butter, ssssss, flip flap.*

Flip flop, flapjack, can you do a flip, Jack?
Hey, butter, batter, butter, flip flap, Jack."

The Little Three weren't eating much. Quinn and Ray are only one and a half, so Mom always tears their pancakes into pieces. Quinn was pounding them flat with his fist, shouting, "Yah! Yah! Yah!" Ray inspected each piece, all concentrating. Then he sucked out the syrup and dropped what was left on the floor for Lucy, the dog.

When they got bored with the pancakes, Quinn and Ray kicked their high chairs.

"Dow! Dow! Dow!" they yelled.

"*Flip flop, flapjack, can you do a flip,*

Jack?" Mom sang louder, to distract Quinn and Ray. She needed to keep the boys locked in so they wouldn't go crashing into furniture and eating crayons and all that stuff babies do when their mother is busy making pancakes.

Lily was at the table, singing, like always:

"Little lizard in my shoe,
Please don't eat my candy cane . . ."

Lily got the singing habit from Mom. Even when Lily's chewing, she at least hums. So she never ends up eating a lot because who can eat and sing at the same time?

But me and Jack and Jenna always eat tons of pancakes. And on the day of Mrs. Kenly, we ate extra tons. We ate until we couldn't take the noise of the twins banging and Lily singing and we went upstairs to play. But my stomach was so packed, I needed to lie down for a minute.

I climbed in my messy bed carefully. When I put a hand on my stomach, it felt like I'd swallowed a balloon.

"Uuuuhhhh . . ." I closed my eyes and hoped my stomach would go back to normal fast.

"Cleo, are you getting ready?" Mom called

from the kitchen. “They’ll be here in twenty minutes.”

“Uuuuuhhhhh . . .”

It was party time.

Chapter 4

I put on the pink dress that used to be Jenna's. I always get her dresses when she gets too big for them. Luckily, my great-aunt Minnie buys me a new dress every spring for my birthday. Otherwise I'd always look like last year's Jenna.

My blue party coat also used to be Jenna's, but it has a velvet collar, so I don't mind.

I love the way that velvet feels on my cheek.

Mr. Kling showed up, like I said, and I got wedged in between Mrs. Kenly and Courtney. Courtney was chewing this gross bubble gum. It smelled watermelon-ish, and she kept blowing giant bubbles. When they popped, *poof*, I'd get a big watermelon breeze in my face. That made my stomach feel REALLY iffy right away.

In the way back, Maddy Goldstein and Emma Fox and Katy were singing:

"*The ants* go *marching one by one,*
hoorah, hoorah,

The ants go marching one by one, hoorah, hoorah,
The ants go marching one by one, the last one stopped to EAT A BUN . . ."

In the next verse, the ants go marching two by two and the last one stops to tie his shoe or whatever you could think of that rhymed. Then they'd go three by three, then four by four, and the song goes on for about a million years. This can be totally fun if you're not in a crowded van and full of pancakes. But after about verse five, the thought of all those black bugs rushing around made me feel even iffier than before.

Plus, Courtney and her mom and dad kept arguing about what to play on the radio. Mr. Kling wanted the football game.

"Naw," Courtney said. "I hate football! And it's my birthday, so I should be radio boss!"

"But . . ." Mr. Kling loves the Chicago Bears.

"Dan, just . . . please," Mrs. Kling chimed in.

So Courtney got to shout “Change!” whenever she wanted to switch the radio station. This happened about every forty-five seconds because they kept landing on commercials.

Some guy yelled about used cars:

"I want YOU, on Michigan Ave-NUE!
Get 'em while they're HOT!
No need to spend a LOT!"

"Change!" (Watermelon breath.)

On the next station, an actress screamed about toothpaste:

"BRUSHA, BRUSH, BRUSH,
DON'T BRUSH IN A RUSH . . . !"

It seems like people on the radio always think they have to yell or you won't hear them.

"Change!"

"Honey, just gimme five minutes, please?" Mr. Kling was desperate.

"Fine!" Courtney said, like it was so NOT fine, but they switched to the game anyway.

"THAT ONE SPLITS THE UP-RIGHTS AND THE BEARS ARE STILL IN THE HUNT FOR THE WILD CARD!"

I wasn't at all sure what the sports announcer meant, but Mr. Kling seemed happy.

"YES!" he shouted.

"Change!" Courtney ordered.

"Aw, baby, just a couple minutes." Mr. Kling was begging now.

Between the radio wars and the ant song and the watermelon gum, I was feeling pretty rocky. I imagined the pancakes in my stomach making faces and complaining, like the twins do when they're trapped in their high chairs.

But what was I going to do, say, "Excuse me, you don't happen to have a bag handy, do you? I need to barf quietly here in the backseat." Or, "Excuse me, can you open the window and let in some air that'll freeze your eyebrows off so I won't throw up and ruin the party?" I mean, I couldn't think of anything to say that wouldn't be just as embarrassing as barfing, so I kept quiet.

I closed my eyes, but that made it worse. I tried to look out the window, but all that stuff whizzing by made it REALLY worse. The pancakes wanted OUT.

Chapter 5

My stomach did a little roll. "Mmmbluh." Of course, I didn't mean to say this; it just popped out.

Mrs. Kenly looked at me. "Are you all right, dear?"

I'm telling you, she's the nicest person in the entire universe, even if she is wearing a coat made out of small brown animals.

"MMMBBluh. I'm fine, thanks."

"You look a little green." Mrs. Kenly's eyebrows went all worried.

I FELT a little green, a LOT green, and when I thought about the color green, I felt even greener.

The ant song got louder:

"THE ANTS GO MARCHING
THIRTEEN BY THIRTEEN,
HOORAH, HOORAH . . ."

Even though I felt about to explode, I wondered what they could possibly rhyme with *thirteen—green*, maybe?

That did it.

"MMMMMMMNDBLLLLL AAAHHHHHHHH!"

It went all over my lap, which was covered with Mrs. Kenly's beautiful fur coat. You could almost hear the little brown animals go, "Awwww, GROSS!" with their mouths all snarly.

But Mrs. Kenly just said, "Oh, dear."

Everybody in the car turned to look, of course, even Mr. Kling, who was driving. He pulled right over. "Oh, my," he said. "You poor kid."

Mrs. Kling said, "My gosh, Sue, your coat."

"Oh, it'll live." Mrs. Kenly gave me a tissue that had pictures of the Eiffel Tower on it and helped me wipe my mouth. I wished I was dead. Well, not dead exactly, but unconscious or on top of the Eiffel Tower, far away.

"Let's get some air, kidlet." Me and Mrs. Kenly got out of the car into the thousand below. Everyone else just kind of stared. Mr.

Kling turned down the volume on the ball game a little, but you could still hear the Bears fans cheering, going wild.

I was so embarrassed, I felt like I was on fire. I wanted them to just leave me there by the road and drive away so I wouldn't have to be in the car, all on fire.

"I'm soooo sorry, Mrs. Kenly." I couldn't look at her.

"It's all right, sweetie, don't worry." Even

though she was the nicest person in the universe, her face looked a little bit like, well, like someone just threw up on her. She dabbed at the mess with another Eiffel Tower tissue.

"Are you all right, honey?" Mrs. Kling asked. "Would you like us to take you home?"

"NOOOO!" I said. I mean, I DID want to go home, of course, so I could lock myself in the bathroom and YELL until the embarrassment went away (which would probably take about fifty years). But I didn't want to cause any more trouble. "I mean, no, thanks, I'm fine. Let's just go." I smiled, but I'm sure it looked really fake.

"Are you sure, kidlet?" Mrs. Kenly asked.

"Yes, thank you. I'll be fine." Yeah, I'll be fine, in about the year 2059.

Back in the van, Emma asked if I was okay and Courtney offered me some watermelon gum.

"Yes, I mean, I'm fine, no, thanks." I smiled some more. (Totally fake.)

We took off and my stomach still felt weird, but I clenched my teeth and sealed my mouth shut: I was SOOO NOT going to barf again.

Chapter 6

Nobody, not even Courtney, complained when Mr. Kling sneaked up the volume on the football game.

"IT'S GOOD FOR FIRST DOWN YARDAGE AND THE BEARS MOVE THE CHAINS AGAIN!"

"Yes! Atta BABY!" Everyone was pretty quiet except Mr. Kling (and the sports announcer). That's 'cause they were all really busy trying to pretend they didn't notice the pukey smell in the car.

I was as embarrassed as if I was sitting there naked with a pumpkin on my head.

It seemed like a year and a half till we got to the club.

The locker room was all pink with a flowery sofa, hair dryers, cotton balls, and shampoo. It had everything you could possibly need if you just threw up on Mrs. Kenly. I could have stayed in there forever, but I put on my bathing suit, which was really Jenna's old one. It was turquoise with little chickens on it, but I so didn't care.

"The ants came marching
fourteen by fourteen,
Hoorah, hoorah . . ."

The other girls started the ant song again. I was glad because then we wouldn't have to talk.

The pool was big and warm, and I was happy to slide into the water and stay under till I thought I would pop.

I thought about Ariel, the Little Mermaid. She would love to be able to go to birthday parties and drive around in vans and chew gum. Right about now I'd switch places with her in a minute, breathe underwater and only talk to fish and never get carsick.

"Let's play Marco Polo!" Courtney yelled.

I played, because I knew I had to pretend I'd forgotten about the barf to get *them* to forget about it.

Mrs. Kenly was sitting by the pool, helping with the lifeguarding and talking with Mrs. Kling. She looked normal, like maybe I hadn't just totally ruined her life or anything. It seemed like she was kind of watching me.

"Hey, Cleo, didn't I hear that you were a diver? Show us a trick, kidlet," she said.

I didn't feel like showing off right now. It was the opposite of what I wanted to do, which was be Ariel the Mermaid. But I couldn't say no to Mrs. Kenly. Also, the diving board was at the other end of the pool away from everyone, which was a plus. I swam all the way there underwater, in one breath.

It was a bouncy board, so a flip was easy. My stomach did a spin when I went over.

"Whoa," said Emma and Maddy and Katy and Courtney.

"Good heavens! Do that again!" Mrs. Kling shouted.

I did it again. Then I did the handstand dive. Everyone had stopped swimming to watch me now, even the strangers. So I did the jackknife, then the swan.

The girls were chanting, "GoooOOO, Cleo! GooooOOOO, CLEO!"

I noticed I wasn't feeling a hundred percent horrible anymore, maybe only sixty-five percent, which was a relief.

"Atta BABY!" Mr. Kling yelled, like I was a Chicago Bear. "First and TEN, do it AGAIN!"

I did another flip.

"AND THE CROWD GOES WILD!" Mr. Kling screamed, and everyone clapped.

I realized I was sort of freezing, so I got out and grabbed one of the poofy towels

from a big neat pile. They all had *Chicago Club* written on them.

All the girls were out by now, wrapped in the Chicago Club towels. Their ponytails and earlobes were dripping when they came over to me.

"Wow, where did you learn that?"

"You are so good of a diver!"

You might think they were trying hard to be nice because of the barf, but I could tell they actually meant all they said.

We sat down for hamburgers and fries, and I told the girls about hairy Mr. Jarvis and how I couldn't dive backward. I didn't eat a lot because I remembered we still had a long drive home.

Mrs. Kling brought out a white cake with about a billion candles on it.

Courtney said we should all help blow them out. I thought, Poor Ariel, she'll never have candles on her cake because there's no fire in the ocean. (Not to mention cake.)

I noticed my smile was back to being real and everybody was acting like nothing ever happened. Well, the diving happened, but not the you-know-what.

Mrs. Kenly put her hand on my shoulder while we watched the presents get opened. Courtney really liked the photo album with the C on it that I gave her, so that was good too.

On the way home, Mrs. Kling let me sit in the front seat. I knew that she knew I'd have less of a chance of throwing up in the front, but she didn't say that, thank goodness. She just told me to sit there. I focused straight ahead.

I felt so much better. I even sang the ant song all the way home. But I was careful to keep my eyes glued on the road in anti-barf position.

They dropped me off and waved good-bye, as if I had never barfed on Mrs. Kenly.

Chapter 7

I could hear Quinn and Ray even before I went in the house, yelling and laughing: "YAAAAHHH ha ha ha! YEEEhee hee!"

"I'm going to EAT YOU ALIVE!" Mom was chasing them with a dragon puppet.

"YAAAAHHH! YAAAAHHH!"

Lily sang quietly in the corner, dancing with a Barbie doll:

"And the tiger caught the mouse,
And he brought her in his house . . ."

Jack and Jenna were in the kitchen, feeding our new bunny, whose name is Captain.

"You have to hold the parsley up over his nose," Jenna was saying.

Dad was fixing the kitchen table for about the eight hundredth time, pounding away with a hammer. "How was the party?" he asked between pounds. But just then, Quinn fell over a toy bulldozer and started screaming, which was good. I mean, not good for Quinn, but good for me because I could sneak upstairs and not answer about the party. I was afraid I'd start feeling lousy again if I did.

I told Mom later, at bedtime.

"Oh, honey, how awful, poor baby . . ."

I cried a little then. Telling Mom about disasters always makes me cry even when I think I'm all back to feeling fine. She started singing:

"The pancakes came marching
six by six, hoorah, hoorah . . ."

I smiled a little.

"The pancakes came marching
six by six, hoorah, hoorah!
The pancakes came marching
six by six,
The last one stopped to do diving
tricks . . ."

We laughed.

Mom hugged me tight.

When she left, I squeezed my eyes shut to squirt out the last, last tear.

Then I did this thing I do sometimes. I thought of what happened that day like it was a story, like a tiny book inside me. In my mind, I lined up the Mrs. Kenly book with the other ones I have in there. There's a little book about when we got caught in a blizzard in Colorado. There's another one about when that giant tortoise got lost in our house. (He was there for my Wild Kingdom birthday party.) There's the story of how I got stitches in my head, and a lot more.

When I'm Mom's age, I'll have so many stories, my insides will look like a library.

Chapter 8

Last night, Mom and Dad had another party with fur coats. Mrs. Kenly came and splashed her coat across the bed with the others. "Hi, kidlets," she said to me and Lily. She whooshed away into the crowded living room.

Later, during Dainty Ladies at the Ball, I put on Mrs. Kenly's coat. I looked at the barf

spot. It was so clean, you'd never have known. What a relief; who knew you could get throw-up out of mink? But maybe a fur coat is easy to clean. Maybe it can have a shampoo, like a dog. I mean, it's small brown animals, after all. And I'm sure they were happy to get the barf washed out of their scalps.